the Pigeon and the Crow

An Indian Folk Tale

RETOLD BY
RUTH MATTISON

ILLUSTRATED BY
MAX STASIUK

PIONEER VALLEY EDUCATIONAL PRESS, INC.

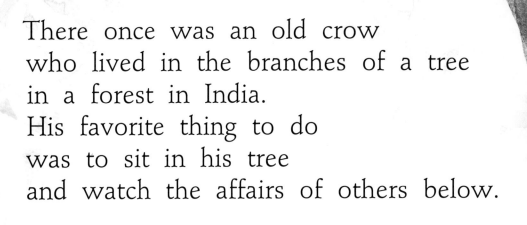

There once was an old crow
who lived in the branches of a tree
in a forest in India.
His favorite thing to do
was to sit in his tree
and watch the affairs of others below.

One day, he looked out
from the leaves of the tree
and noticed a man. The man was
walking along the path
carrying a large stick in one hand
and a net in the other.

"That fellow is up to some mischief,"
thought the crow.
"I will keep my eye on him."

The man stopped under the tree
and spread the net on the ground.
Next, he took a bag of rice
out of his pocket
and scattered the grains of rice
over his net. Then he hid
behind the trunk of the crow's tree.

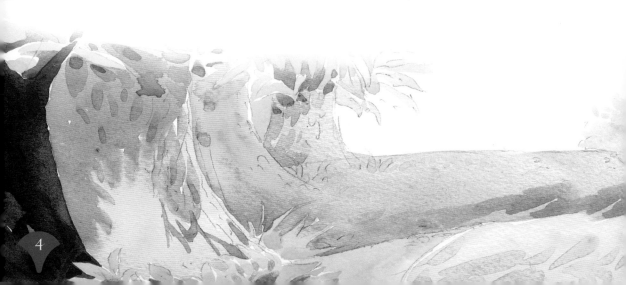

"I wonder what he is up to,"
thought the crow, watching the net.
"Could the man have some plans
for the birds? I have a nasty feeling
about that stick!"

The crow was quite right,
and it was not long
before just what he expected
came to pass.

A large pigeon with colorful plumage
came flying along. A flock of smaller
pigeons followed him. They noticed the rice,
but did not see the net.

The large pigeon and his companions
swept down, eager to enjoy
an unexpected meal of rice.
Alas, their joy was short lived.
Their feet became trapped in the net
as they were eating.

"Coo! Coo!" they called in distress
as they struggled to escape.

The crow watched as the man got ready
to step out of hiding and beat
the poor, helpless pigeons with his stick.
But then something surprising happened.

The largest of the pigeons
said to the others,
"Take the net in your beaks,
and spread out your wings.
Then fly straight up into the air
as quickly as you can."

Each little pigeon did as it was told
and seized a separate thread
of the net in its beak. Up, up, up
they all flew, looking very beautiful
with the sunlight gleaming
on their white wings. Very soon,
they were out of sight.

The man with the stick
stepped out from behind the tree,
looking quite surprised
at what had happened.
He stood gazing up at his net
as it disappeared up into the sky.
Muttering under his breath, he went
down the path towards town.

The old crow chuckled.
He found it quite enjoyable
to see the birds outwit the man.

11

When the pigeons had flown
some distance, they stopped
to rest awhile in a clearing
of the forest. They lay
on the ground panting for breath.

The largest pigeon said,
"I have been thinking
about what we can do to free ourselves.
I have come up with an idea.
We will take this horrible net
to my old friend the mouse.
He can nibble through the strings
and set us all free.

"Unfortunately, he lives back in the big tree
   where we found the rice,"
   the large pigeon sighed.
"We'll have to fly back there
   and ask him for help."

So the weary pigeons picked up the net
and flew back to the path in the forest
where they had been caught.

13

The crow was quite surprised
to see the pigeons return
and stop just beneath his tree.

"Coo! Coo!" cried the pigeons.

"Who are they calling to?"
wondered the crow. He watched
as a mouse popped out of a little hole.

"Why, they were calling to the mouse who lives at the bottom of my tree!" thought the crow. "What good can he do?"

The mouse began to nibble on the strings of the net, and the crow thought, "Ah! I see! That large pigeon is a very smart and sensible bird!"

Very soon, the mouse
had freed the pigeons.

"A friend in need is a friend indeed,"
cried the largest pigeon.
"Many thanks to you, little mouse!"
And the pigeons flew
up into the beautiful sky, happy to be free.

From then on, all of those birds
remembered their adventure
and never picked up food from the ground
without a good look at it first.